HORSEBACK
Hopes

BY JAKE MADDOX

illustrated by Tuesday Mourning

text by Diana G. Gallagher

Impact Books are published by Stone Arch Books,
A Capstone Imprint
151 Good Counsel Drive, P.O. Box 669
Mankato, Minnesota 56002
www.capstonepub.com

Library of Congress Cataloging-in-Publication Data
Maddox, Jake.
    Horseback Hopes / by Jake Maddox; illustrated by Tuesday
Mourning.
        p. cm. — (Impact Books. A Jake Maddox Sports Story)
        ISBN 978-1-4342-1214-6 (library binding)
        ISBN 978-1-4342-1401-0 (pbk.)
        [1. Horsemanship—Fiction.] I. Mourning, Tuesday, ill. II. Title.
PZ7.M25643Ho 2009
[Fic]—dc22   2008031957

Summary:
Molly has always dreamed of taking horseback riding lessons, but the
lessons were too expensive. Until now! A new stable has opened up in
town, and Molly convinces her parents to let her sign up for classes.
Everything is great . . . except that two girls at school keep making fun
of Molly. She'll need to figure out a way to keep her confidence both in
and out of the saddle.

Creative Director: Heather Kindseth
Graphic Designer: Carla Zetina-Yglesias

Photo Credits:
iStock/Sam Sefton, cover (background), 1 (background)

Printed in the United States of America in Stevens Point, Wisconsin.
                            062010
                          005865R

Table of Contents

A New Stable

Molly Burke stopped walking and stared at the new flyer on the school bulletin board. "Pinch me, Kari," she said.

"Why?" her best friend asked.

"So I know I'm not dreaming," Molly said. She rubbed her eyes and looked again.

She wasn't dreaming. The flyer said, "North Star Stable: Horseback Riding Lessons, Low Prices."

Kari looked at the flyer and sighed. "Oh," she said. "Horseback riding lessons. I was hoping it was going to be something exciting."

"It is exciting!" Molly said.

Molly had loved horses since the first time she saw one on TV. She cut horse pictures out of magazines and saved them in a scrapbook. She had read all the horse books in the library, twice!

She collected glass horses and horse toys. The bouncy-horse she had when she was little was still stored in the attic. But she'd never ridden on a real horse.

"This could totally change my life," Molly said.

"I thought your dad wouldn't let you take lessons," Kari said.

"He won't let me take lessons at Bay Meadow," Molly said. "Too expensive. But this says low prices!"

Kari leaned closer to read the small print on the flyer. "The trainer is a fifth-grade teacher," she told Molly. "Her name is Ms. North."

Molly smiled. "That will make it even easier to convince my parents to let me take lessons," she said. "Where is this new stable?"

Gabrielle and Lily walked up behind them. Molly spun around.

"What new stable?" Gabrielle asked, crossing her arms.

Molly looked at the flyer and read the address. "It says it's on Skylark Road," she said.

"I know that place. It's next to Bay Meadow," Lily said. "It's not a new stable. It's an old farm." She and Gabrielle looked at each other and laughed.

Molly frowned. She knew that Gabrielle and Lily kept their horses at Bay Meadow. They wore riding clothes to school when they had horse shows, which Molly thought was really cool.

Molly had always wanted to be friends with Gabrielle and Lily, since they loved horses as much as she did. But Gabrielle and Lily didn't want to be friends with her. They only hung out with kids who took lessons at Bay Meadow and owned horses of their own.

"I can't believe somebody bought that rundown place," Gabrielle added.

"Maybe Ms. North fixed it up," Kari said.

"Maybe, but I bet the horses are old and boring," Gabrielle said. "Lesson horses usually are. That's why Lily and I own our own horses. Taking lessons at some old farm really isn't the same thing at all." She stuck her nose in the air. Then Gabrielle and Lily walked away.

Molly frowned. But she didn't care if it wasn't the same. She just wanted to learn how to ride a horse. As long as it had four legs, a mane, and a tail, any horse would be perfect.

Molly looked at the flyer. Then she wrote down the phone number in her notebook.

Dream Come True

At dinner, Molly waited until her older brother, Ken, finished talking to their parents about baseball practice. Then she blurted out her news.

"A new stable just opened up on Skylark Road," Molly said quickly. "The trainer is a fifth-grade teacher, and it's cheaper than Bay Meadow. Can I take riding lessons there?"

Her mom frowned. "That's a long way from here," Mom said. "You can't walk."

"I can ride my bike," Molly said. She rode her bike to school sometimes, and that was farther than the stable was.

"I can drive her," Ken offered.

Molly smiled. Ken was sixteen. He had just passed his driver's test, and he'd do anything to drive the family car.

"Do you know the teacher's name?" her mom asked.

"Ms. North," Molly said. "I wrote down the phone number."

Molly's mom and dad looked at each other.

"We'll think about it," her dad said finally. "Mom and I will talk after dinner."

After dinner, Molly went to her room to do her homework. She couldn't keep her mind on math and history. All she could think about was horses. Molly wanted to learn to ride more than anything.

An hour later, there was a knock on Molly's bedroom door. Her mom walked in.

"Well, I talked to the trainer," Molly's mom said. She sat on the edge of Molly's bed and added, "Ms. North was very nice and answered all our questions."

"And?" Molly asked. She held her breath.

"Your father and I decided that we will pay for ten group lessons," her mom said. "Ms. North has a special rate for new students, and she'll give us a refund if you don't like it."

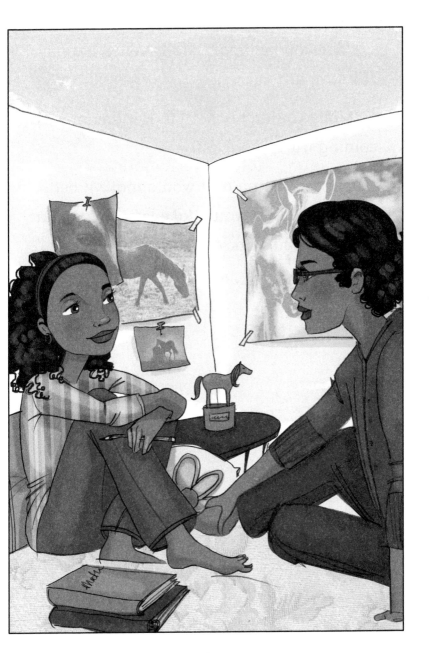

"Are you kidding?" Molly yelled happily. "I'll love it!"

Molly couldn't believe it. Her dream was coming true.

The only thing that would make it better would be if Kari would take lessons too. But Kari didn't like horses.

It didn't matter. Molly was finally going to learn to ride.

First Lesson

Molly's first lesson was a few days later. She had begged Kari to come watch her first lesson, and Kari had finally given in. They rode their bikes to the stable together after school.

Molly had already changed into her new riding clothes. She was wearing long pants and boots. The boots would make sure that her feet wouldn't slip through the stirrups while she was riding.

"This is it. Your big day," Kari said as they walked together toward the barn. "Are you excited?"

"Yep," Molly said with a nervous smile. "I'm so excited! I can't wait. My knees are shaking."

"Look at that!" Kari said, pointing to the field on the other side of the fence. A horse and rider galloped toward a tall hedge and jumped it.

"I wouldn't do that in a million years," Kari said. "Not even for a million dollars."

"I would!" Molly exclaimed. "I hope I can ride like that someday."

They walked inside the barn. Kari sat on a bench by the barn door, and Molly joined the other kids. There were two girls and one boy.

A woman stepped forward. "You must be Molly Burke," she said. "I'm Ms. North. Everyone is here now, so we can get started!"

Ms. North led a big gray horse out of a stall and clipped two ropes to his halter. "Riding is only part of good horsemanship," she said. "Before you ride, you have to groom the horse."

Molly paid close attention as Ms. North moved a rubber curry-comb in slow circles over the horse's neck, sides, and rump.

"Does he like that?" Molly asked. "It kind of looks like it would hurt."

Ms. North laughed. "It doesn't hurt at all. Casper loves it," she said. "He loves it almost as much as he likes hay and oats. And he likes hay and oats a lot."

Ms. North brushed the loose dirt off Casper. Then she used a cloth to make his coat shine. Finally, the trainer combed Casper's mane and tail with a metal comb and untangled the snags with her fingers. Molly watched carefully.

"Who wants to clean his hooves?" Ms. North asked. "Casper is old and lazy. He won't kick."

Molly was the only one who raised her hand. "I will," she said.

"Great, Molly," Ms. North said. "Come on up. I'll show you what to do."

Molly did exactly what Ms. North told her. When Molly touched the back of Casper's lower leg, he lifted his foot. Then she held his hoof and picked the dirt out with a metal hook tool.

"Very good, Molly!" Ms. North said, smiling. "A horse with a stone in his hoof is like a car with a flat tire. It can't go very far." The teacher saddled and bridled Casper. "I'll teach you how to tack up next time," she said.

"Tack something up on a bulletin board?" the boy asked. The girls laughed.

"Saddles and bridles are tack, Max," Ms. North explained. "Tacking up means putting them on the horse." She gave Casper's reins to Molly and said, "Take Casper to the riding ring."

Molly put one hand on the reins under Casper's chin and held the long ends of the reins in the other hand. She stayed on the left by his head. She had to tug on the reins and make a clucking noise to get Casper to move.

Kari hurried out of the barn ahead of them. "Horses sure are a lot of work," she said. "We've been here for half an hour, and you haven't even ridden one yet!"

"I think this part is fun too," Molly said, patting Casper's neck. "Hey, touch his nose," she told Molly. "It's so soft and warm."

Kari shuddered. "No way," she said.

The students led their horses into the ring and lined up in the middle. Ms. North helped everyone get on. As soon as Molly was aboard Casper, she grabbed the front of the saddle. It was a long way down!

"Remember," Ms. North said, "horses are bigger, but people are smarter. So never blame the horse when something goes wrong, even if it is his fault!"

Molly giggled. She was starting to feel more relaxed.

Ms. North stood in the center of the ring and explained the basics of good form. "Sit up straight," she told the class. "Keep your elbows in and your heels down. To make the horse walk, tighten your reins and squeeze your legs."

Molly squeezed her legs, but Casper didn't move.

"Just kick him with your heel, Molly!" Ms. North said.

Molly kicked, and the big horse started walking — straight toward the fence! Molly panicked. Was the horse going to keep walking and crash into the fence? It didn't seem like he was going to stop.

"What do I do?" she yelled.

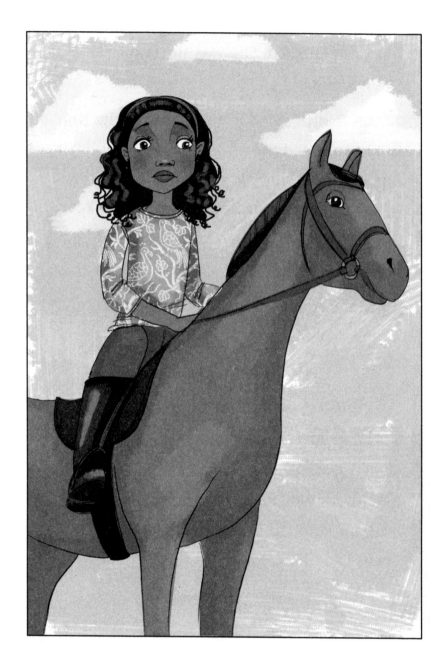

"Pull back on the left rein," Ms. North told her. "Don't pull out! Pull back!"

Molly pulled back on the rein in her left hand. Casper turned to the left and walked next to the fence. "Good job," Ms. North called.

The other three horses were faster. Molly couldn't get Casper to speed up.

"You're all hunched over!" Kari said as Molly passed her. "And your reins are too loose."

When Molly shortened her reins and sat up straighter, Casper decided to catch up to the other horses. He broke into a slow trot, and Molly bounced up and down.

"Pull back on the reins to make him walk," Ms. North said. "And keep those heels down, Molly."

Molly flopped around like a rag doll, but she got Casper to walk again. Then she heard someone laugh. She looked over the fence.

Gabrielle and Lily were riding in the Bay Meadow field. Their sleek horses pranced quickly, but both girls rode like they were glued to their saddles. They slowed down and watched Molly for a moment. Then they giggled again.

Molly's cheeks flushed. She was pretty embarrassed, but she was determined to get it right. After all, Gabrielle and Lily had been beginners once. If they could learn to ride, so could she.

Aches and Pains

The next morning, Molly woke up stiff and sore. Her muscles ached so much that it hurt to even brush her teeth. After she got dressed, she limped into the kitchen. Her family was already at the table.

"What's wrong?" Mom asked. She poured Molly a glass of orange juice.

"My whole body hurts," Molly moaned.

"That's because riding uses muscles you haven't used before," her father said.

"No pain, no gain," Ken added. "That's what my football coach always says."

"My next lesson is in two days," Molly said. "How can I ride if I can hardly walk?"

"Take a hot bath after school," her mother suggested. "That might help."

"How did the riding go yesterday?" Dad asked.

"It wasn't what I expected," Molly said. "I thought I could just hop on and gallop off, but riding a horse is harder than it looks."

Her mother gasped. "Did the horse try to run away with you?" she asked nervously.

"No!" Molly said. She rolled her eyes and laughed. "The horse I rode only has two speeds. Slow and very slow."

"Good," Mom said, looking relieved. She paused. Then she said, "I know we've always said you have to finish what you start, but we won't be mad if you want to quit riding."

"Quit? No way!" Molly exclaimed. She ached all over, and old Casper was slow, but Molly was already in love with horseback riding!

* * *

On the way to school, Molly started worrying. She wanted to ask Kari to come along to the next lesson, but Molly was pretty sure Kari had been bored during the riding class.

What if Kari didn't want to go again? Molly knew that riding wouldn't be as much fun without her best friend.

Molly didn't say anything about it until they sat down for lunch. Then she asked Kari, "Are you busy Saturday?"

"I don't think so," Kari said. "Why?"

"I really want you to come to my next lesson," Molly said. "It'll make me less nervous if you're there."

Just then, Gabrielle and Lily walked by with their lunch trays. They stopped and looked at Molly.

"You'll never learn to ride on that old horse you were riding yesterday," Lily said. "He's so old I bet he can't even stand up for ten minutes at a time."

The insult made Molly mad, but she didn't want Lily and Gabrielle to know. "Casper is quiet and calm," Molly told them. "That's why he's good for beginners."

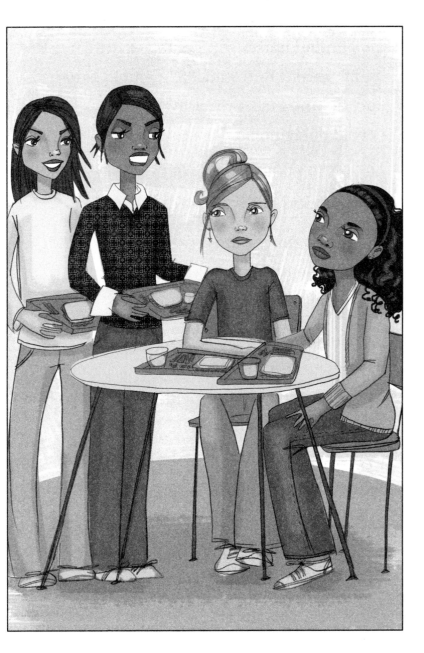

"Young horses can get too excited sometimes," Kari said. "Sometimes they act up and buck or run away. Casper is a dependable horse."

Molly blinked. *When did Kari become a horse expert?* she wondered.

"Good point, Kari," Gabrielle said. "It'll be a long time before Molly can handle a show horse like Rebel Wings."

Gabrielle's horse, Rebel Wings, was a junior jumper. Jumpers had to get over fences without knocking down rails. Points were taken off if a rail fell. Points were called faults, and a round with no faults was perfect. If more than one horse had zero faults, the fastest horse won.

Lily laughed. "There's no way Molly would ever be able to ride Jubilee," she said meanly.

Lily's horse, Jubilee, was a junior hunter. Hunters had to get over the jumps and mind their manners. If a hunter bucked, it didn't win.

"We're riding in the Bay Meadows Junior Horse Show next week," Lily added.

"That sounds like fun," Molly said, "but you're right, Gabrielle. Rebel Wings is too nervous for me. I'm working really hard, though. I want to ride as well as you someday."

Molly could tell that the compliment surprised Gabrielle. Gabrielle just opened her mouth and then closed it again. Finally, she just mumbled, "Thanks."

Lily and Gabrielle walked away. Then Molly looked at Kari and asked, "When did you learn so much about horses?"

"I listened to everything Ms. North told you," Kari said. "Riding is a lot more interesting than I thought it would be."

Molly grinned. "Does that mean you want to ride?" she asked.

"No!" Kari said loudly. She shook her head. "Absolutely not. But I will go to your lesson on Saturday."

"Great!" Molly said. But she was starting to realize something. Kari, who was usually not afraid of anything, was afraid of horses!

Trail Trouble

Kari went to every lesson with Molly for two weeks. Kari watched the class ride, played with Ms. North's dog, and petted the barn cat. But no matter what, she wouldn't ever touch a horse.

Molly liked having Kari's company at the stable, so she didn't tease her friend about being afraid of horses. Molly understood. After all, horses were really big! Molly loved them, but Kari didn't have to.

"I offered to feed the horses and do the barn chores at North Star today," Molly told Kari one Monday. "Kids who help out get extra riding time. Ms. North has parent-teacher meetings after school. Do you want to help?"

"Sure," Kari said, "but I'm not going anywhere near the stalls."

"You won't have to," Molly said. "Promise."

After school, Ken drove Molly and Kari to the stable. When Molly walked into the barn, she felt really nervous. Even though Ms. North had shown Molly what to do, she was nervous about doing the chores on her own. She didn't want to mess anything up.

"Where do we start?" Kari asked. She followed Molly into the tack room.

Rows of saddle and bridle racks covered the walls. Three dirty bridles hung down from a hook on the ceiling.

Molly pointed at the bridles. "Let's clean tack," she said.

"I'll get the hot water," Kari said.

Kari filled a bucket at the sink and set it down. Molly unhooked the bridles. Then Kari washed dried grass off the metal bits. When she finished cleaning the bits, she put the bridles back on the hook.

Molly rubbed a bar of orange saddle soap with a wet sponge and cleaned the leather straps. After she rinsed off the soap with another sponge, Kari dried the straps with a cloth and rubbed in leather conditioner. Finally, they hung the clean bridles on the wall.

Kari dumped the dirty water in the sink and put the bucket away. "I don't know why," she said, "but I don't mind cleaning here. Even though I hate it at home."

"I know," Molly said. "I feel the same way. I hate cleaning at home too, but here, it's sort of fun!"

Kari smiled. "Now what?" she asked.

"I'll get the hay, and you fill the water buckets," Molly said.

"Sounds good," Kari said, smiling. She pulled a hose over to Casper's stall. Standing outside the stall, she stuck the hose through the bars into his bucket and filled it up.

Molly headed outside to the hay bales. She wasn't strong enough to drag a whole bale of hay into the barn.

Instead, Molly peeled off sections and put them in a wheelbarrow. Then she carted the hay inside.

The horses didn't try to leave when Molly opened the stall doors. They knew it was time for dinner. She tossed a large clump into the corner of every stall.

"Do we have to feed them anything else?" Kari asked.

"Nope," Molly told her. "Ms. North said she'd give them the rest of their food when she gets home."

"So what's next?" Kari asked.

"We have to muck out," Molly said. "You know, get the gross stuff out of the stalls."

"I don't want to muck out," Kari said. "I'll sweep."

"Works for me," Molly said.

She used a pitchfork and a huge plastic bucket to take wet straw and manure out of every stall. Ms. North cleaned the stalls really well every morning, so there wasn't much.

Kari stood back to admire the floor. She had swept up every bit of hay and dirt on the cement. "Is that it?" she asked.

"Just about," Molly said. She quickly checked the stall doors to make sure they were latched. "Now we're done," she said.

The two girls walked outside and sat on the fence to wait for Ken to pick them up. A few minutes later, Gabrielle rode by on Rebel Wings.

"Hi, Gabrielle," Molly said. "Where's Lily?"

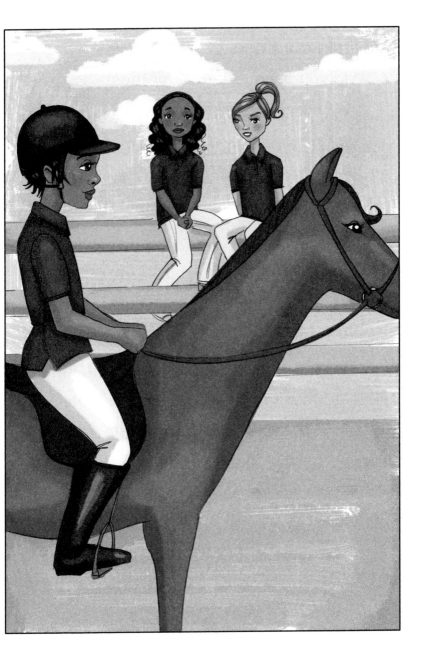

"She's at the dentist," Gabrielle said. "Will you open that gate for me?"

Molly opened the gate to the trails. Gabrielle rode through. As the horse and rider turned toward the woods, Molly frowned. She called out, "It's not safe to ride on the trails alone!"

Gabrielle didn't look back. She trotted Rebel Wings down the bridle path and disappeared into the trees.

"I'm sure she'll be fine," Kari said. But Molly wasn't so sure. And a few minutes later, they heard Gabrielle scream.

Risky Rescue

"Something's wrong," Molly said.

"I'll go call Ms. North," Kari said. She headed for the barn. "I saw a phone in the tack room."

"Ms. North is too far away," Molly said, running ahead. "I'm going to get Casper and go find Gabrielle." She opened the barn door and went inside.

"You can't take a horse out alone!" Kari exclaimed.

"I know, but this is an emergency," Molly said. She took a deep breath and looked Kari in the eye. "You'll have to hold Casper while I get on."

Kari gasped. "No way," she said.

"Kari, you have to," Molly said. "I need your help. And so does Gabrielle."

"But what if he bites me?" Kari asked nervously. "Or kicks me? Or steps on my foot or something? I really can't touch that horse."

"He won't do anything," Molly said. "Come on. If Gabrielle is hurt, we have to help her."

Kari took a deep breath. "Fine," she said. She got Casper's saddle and bridle from the tack room. Then she stood back as Molly took Casper out of his stall.

Molly had to hurry, so she only had time to quickly brush the horse's back and check his feet for stones. After she put Casper's saddle on, she led him outside. Kari slowly followed.

"This isn't hard, Kari," Molly said. "Just hold the reins tight under his chin so he can't walk away."

Kari slowly walked up to the horse. Her hand shook when she took the reins. Molly knew that would make some horses nervous, but Casper didn't even twitch.

"What if he moves?" Kari asked.

"Pull back and say 'whoa!'," Molly told her.

Molly stretched to get her left foot in the stirrup. Then she grabbed the saddle, hopped, and pulled herself up.

"Okay. I'm on," she said.

Kari gave Casper a quick pat on the neck and stepped back. "Good luck," she told Molly.

Molly turned Casper down the bridle path and kicked him into a trot.

The trail through the woods was pretty, but Molly was too worried about Gabrielle to enjoy it. After a few minutes, she pulled Casper back to a slow trot. She didn't want to move too quickly, in case she had to duck under a tree branch.

"Gabrielle!" Molly yelled. "Gabrielle!"

"I'm over here!" Gabrielle called.

Molly trotted Casper forward. Soon, she spotted Gabrielle sitting on a big log.

"What happened?" Molly asked.

Gabrielle stood up and brushed off her pants. She had dirt on her face, but she didn't look hurt. "A stupid squirrel scared Rebel," she said. "He moved back, and I fell off."

"Where is Rebel?" Molly asked.

"He ran away," Gabrielle said. "I tried to catch him, but he's too fast. I'm really worried."

"Casper's not speedy, but he goes faster than we can," Molly told her. She moved the horse over to the log and said, "Get on behind me."

Gabrielle frowned and asked, "Are you sure he rides double? If he can only handle one rider, this is a really bad idea."

"It's fine," Molly said. "Nothing bothers Casper."

After Gabrielle got on, Molly kicked Casper into a slow jog. Both girls searched the woods for the lost horse.

After a few minutes, Gabrielle gasped. "There he is!" she said, pointing ahead.

Rebel's reins were tangled in a patch of bushes. He was breathing hard, and sweat covered his coat. He was stuck, scared, and tired.

Gabrielle slid to the ground. She moved slowly toward Rebel, talking softly as she walked.

"Easy, boy. It's okay," she said quietly. She untangled the reins and led Rebel out of the brush. Then she carefully got on his back.

"Are you sure you're okay?" Molly asked.

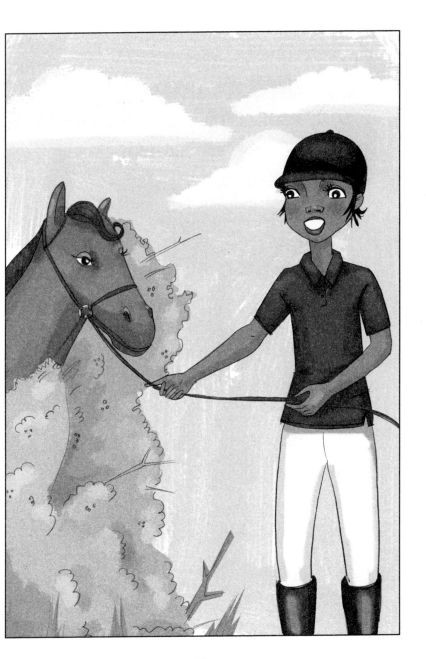

"Yeah. Thanks," Gabrielle said. She turned and rode back toward the barn.

Molly frowned. Then she patted Casper's neck. "Good boy," she said softly. "You saved the day."

Horse Show

A few weeks later, Molly grinned as she looked out over the Bay Meadow Junior Horse Show.

Trucks and horse trailers were parked in one field. Red, white, and blue jumps were set up in the large show area. Young riders were brushing horses or riding in the warm-up ring. They all wore velvet hard hats, breeches, and shiny boots. Some were also wearing hunt coats and shirts with wide collars.

"I can't believe we're here!" Molly exclaimed.

"It would be more fun if you were showing," Kari said.

"Yeah, but there's an entry fee for every class," Molly explained. "I didn't want to ask my parents for more money. We'll still have fun helping the other kids."

Four of Ms. North's other students were riding in beginner groups. Molly and Kari had come to watch, work, and learn.

Ms. North walked Casper down the ramp of her horse trailer.

"Kari, can you hold Casper for a few minutes?" Ms. North asked. "It's okay to let him eat grass."

"Sure," Kari said. She took the lead rope and led Casper to a patch of green grass.

Molly smiled. Kari still didn't want to ride, but she liked taking care of the gentle old horse.

"Molly, will you take these entry forms and fees to the show tent?" Ms. North asked. She pointed toward the arena. "They'll give you number cards for our riders."

"Sure," Molly said. "Be right back!"

She hurried to the tent. After she handed in the forms, she wrote each rider's name on a number card. Every rider would wear a different number.

While Ms. North's students practiced, Molly and Kari watched the other riders. In the first group, the riders were asked to walk, trot, and canter. The judge scored the riders on how well they rode.

In other groups, like Gabrielle's junior jumper group and Lily's hunter group, the judge scored the horses, not the riders.

Molly and Kari watched as Gabrielle entered the ring and eased her horse into a canter. Then it was time for the jumps. The jumps were made of rails, white gates, and bushes.

Rebel Wings cleared every jump without knocking anything down. Molly clapped and cheered when he won a blue ribbon for first place.

In the hunter group, Lily's horse cleared every fence, but hunters were also judged on looks, gait, and manners. Jubilee won a yellow ribbon for third place.

"We'd better get back," Kari said. "I promised to help Max get Casper ready."

When they got back to the trailer, Max was sitting on the ramp. He didn't look happy.

"What's wrong, Max?" Molly asked.

"I don't want to show," Max said. "I bounce around too much. It's really embarrassing."

"It's okay, Max," Ms. North said, smiling. "Horse shows should be fun. You don't have to ride if you don't want to."

"Molly knows how to walk and trot," Kari said. "She could show instead."

"Yeah, let Molly ride!" Max said. "Then it's not a waste of my entry fee. That will make my mom happy."

"I can't be in the show!" Molly exclaimed. "I didn't bring my riding clothes."

"You're right. That is a problem," Ms. North said. "I have an extra hard hat, but you need breeches and boots."

"Could we borrow some?" Kari asked.

Molly looked at the other North Star kids. They were all younger, and their clothes were too small. She really wanted to ride, but she couldn't do it without the right clothes. The horse show had strict rules.

"Don't give up," Ms. North said. "Tack up Casper, and I'll check with the other trainers. Someone must have clothes in your size that we can use."

Molly and Kari each brushed one side of the horse. Kari combed out his mane and tail, and Molly polished his hooves with oil to make them shine. Then they saddled and bridled him.

Soon, Ms. North was back, frowning. "Sorry, Molly. No luck," she said.

Molly put down the brush she'd been using to smooth Casper's coat. "Thanks for trying," she said. She smiled, but she felt really disappointed.

Then she heard a shout. "Molly!"

Molly looked up. Gabrielle and Lily were running toward her. "I heard you had a problem," Gabrielle said.

Molly nodded. "I can't ride in the walk-trot class because I didn't bring my riding gear," she explained.

"We always bring an extra set of clothes," Lily said.

"In case we fall in the dirt or it rains," Gabrielle said. "You can borrow my clothes," she added. "They should fit you."

"Really?" Molly said.

Gabrielle shrugged and smiled. "I owe you a favor," she explained. She handed a bundle of clothes to Molly.

Kari looked at her watch. "You only have ten minutes!" she said. "Go change, Molly. I'll take Casper to the arena!"

The Great Casper

Ms. North pinned a number card to the back of Molly's coat. Then she gave her a boost onto Casper's back.

Molly was nervous. "I don't want to mess up," she admitted.

"You'll be fine," Ms. North said. "Casper knows what to do."

Molly looked over to the fence nearby, where her teammates were watching. Lily and Gabrielle were there too.

"Good luck," Lily said. She gave Molly a thumbs-up.

"I hope you win a ribbon," Gabrielle said.

"Did you win a ribbon in your first horse show?" Kari asked.

"Yep," Gabrielle said. She grinned. "I came in sixth. Out of six."

Molly counted the horses waiting at the gate. Twelve. Six ribbons would be awarded, so she had a fifty-fifty chance. Winning would be nice, but she was just glad to be riding in the show.

As the other riders moved into the ring, Ms. North gave Molly some advice. "Stay close to the fence," Ms. North said. "Don't get bunched up with the other horses."

"Okay," Molly said.

She shortened her reins, sat up straight, and entered the arena. The minute the gate closed, Casper's ears perked up. He walked a little faster and picked up his feet. Molly smiled. She knew that Casper was showing off for the judges.

"Walk!" the announcer said over the loudspeakers.

Ms. North stood by the fence. "You're looking good, Molly!" she called. "Push those heels down."

Molly pushed her heels down and looked straight ahead.

"Trot!" the announcer said. Casper started trotting.

Kari was standing on the opposite side of the big show ring. As Molly rode by, Kari yelled, "Elbows in!"

Molly tucked in her elbows. There was so much to remember. She was glad to have a second coach.

"Walk," the announcer said, "and reverse."

Molly turned Casper toward the center of the ring and changed directions. She smiled.

Then she realized that she'd stopped being nervous. In fact, she'd started enjoying herself.

The announcer ran through the same set of instructions again. When the group trotted, two horses rushed up behind Casper. They passed too close, startling Molly. She tensed, but Casper kept going like nothing had happened.

"Walk!" the announcer called.

That was it. It was over.

Kari smiled when Molly and Casper walked by. "You were fantastic!" she said.

"Thanks for the help," Molly said. "It was fun. You should try riding sometime."

"Maybe I will," Kari said. "Ms. North said that you're good enough to ride Rainbow now, so maybe I can try riding Casper."

Molly was thrilled. Things couldn't get much better. Rainbow was Ms. North's best horse, and Kari wanted to ride!

"Line up, please," the announcer said.

Molly rode into the center of the arena. The riders lined up side by side. The judge walked behind them and wrote the winning numbers on his clipboard. Then he handed the clipboard to the announcer.

A few horses jiggled while they waited. Casper stood still, and Molly patted him on the neck. He was the perfect horse for her first show. She knew she wouldn't win, but she'd had a great time.

The announcer called out first and second place. The riders rode up to the judge, who handed them blue and red ribbons. Then the announcer said, "Third place goes to Molly Burke on Casper."

Molly's jaw dropped. "What?" she said. Then she heard cheering coming from her friends near the fence.

Molly smiled. Then she rode Casper over to the judge and accepted her first ribbon.

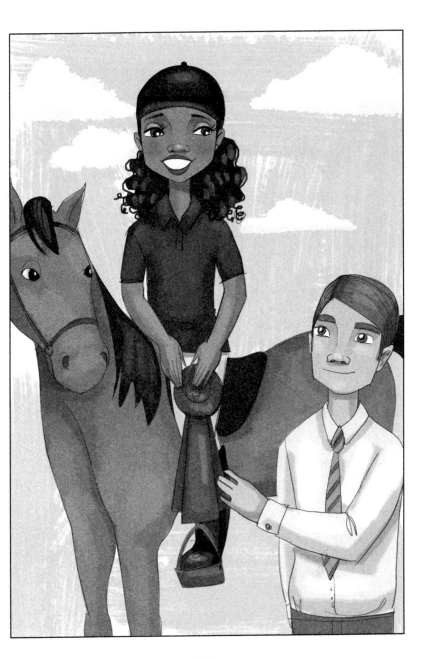

ABOUT THE AUTHOR

Diana G. Gallagher lives in Florida with her husband and five dogs, four cats, and a cranky parrot. She has been an English equitation instructor, a professional folk musician, and an artist. However, she had aspirations to be a professional writer at the age of twelve. She has written dozens of books for kids and young adults.

ABOUT THE ILLUSTRATOR

When Tuesday Mourning was a little girl, she knew she wanted to be an artist when she grew up. Now, she is an illustrator who lives in Knoxville, Tennessee. She especially loves illustrating books for kids and teenagers. When she isn't illustrating, Tuesday loves spending time with her husband, who is an actor, and their son, Atticus.

GLOSSARY

breeches (BREECH-iz)—knee-length pants that are tight at the bottom

canter (KAN-tur)—when a horse canters, it runs at a speed between a trot and a gallop

curry-comb (KUH-ree-kohm)—a special brush used for cleaning horses

dependable (di-PEN-duh-buhl)—if someone is dependable, you can rely on them

emergency (ee-MUR-juhn-see)—a dangerous situation that must be handled right away

gallop (GAL-uhp)—when a horse gallops, it runs as fast as it can

groom (GROOM)—to brush and clean a horse

reins (RAYNZ)—straps that help control a horse

stable (STAY-buhl)—a place where horses are kept

stirrups (STIR-uhps)—loops that hang down from a saddle, where a rider's feet go

trot (TROT)—when a horse trots, it moves quickly but more slowly than when it canters

MORE ABOUT HORSEBACK RIDING

Learning how to ride a horse takes time. It also takes proper training. However, it does not take much equipment. You don't need your own horse, and you certainly don't need fancy clothes.

A beginning rider will need:

- a pair of sturdy boots with a low heel

- comfortable pants

- good gloves

- a riding helmet

The horse, saddle, and other equipment should be available at the stables.

The best place to learn to ride is at a riding school. Look for a school that has clean stables and healthy horses. Also make sure that the school has qualified instructors and small class sizes.

At a riding school, you will learn how to properly groom and ride a horse. To find a good riding school in your area, check with the Pony Club. (You can search online for the Pony Club, or ask a parent or teacher for help.)

It takes time to build a relationship with a horse. You must be patient. With training and time, a horse can become a great friend.

DISCUSSION QUESTIONS

1. Why were Gabrielle and Lily mean to Molly at the beginning of this book? Do you think Molly handled it correctly?

2. In chapter 6, Molly takes a risk when she rides into the woods alone to help Gabrielle. Do you think she did the right thing? Why or why not? What else could she have done to help Gabrielle?

3. What other books, stories, movies, or TV shows do you know about horseback riding? Talk about other things you know about horseback riding.

WRITING PROMPTS

1. Molly has always wanted to be able to take horseback riding lessons. Write about something you have always wanted to do.

2. Molly's best friend, Kari, goes to Molly's riding lessons even though Kari isn't interested in riding. Write about a time you did something your best friend wanted to do, even though you weren't interested.

3. At the end of this book, Molly wins a ribbon. Write about a time that you won something. What did you do? What did you win?

INTERNET SITES

Do you want to know more about subjects related to this book? Or are you interested in learning about other topics? Then check out FactHound, a fun, easy way to find Internet sites.

Our investigative staff has already sniffed out great sites for you!

Here's how to use FactHound:

1. Visit *www.facthound.com*

2. Select your grade level.

3. To learn more about subjects related to this book, type in the book's ISBN number: **9781434212146**.

4. Click the **Fetch It** button.

FactHound will fetch the best Internet sites for you!